THE SCIENCE OF THE BEAST
The Facts Behind the Fangs

THE MAKING OF A MONSTER

Vampires & Werewolves

THE SCIENCE OF THE BEAST

The Facts Behind
the Fangs

by Kim Etingoff

Mason Crest Publishers

MASON CREST PUBLISHERS INC.
370 Reed Road
Broomall, Pennsylvania 19008
(866)MCP-BOOK (toll free)
www.masoncrest.com

First Printing
9 8 7 6 5 4 3 2 1

ISBN (series) 978-1-4222-1801-3
Paperback ISBN (series) 978-1-4222-1954-6

Library of Congress Cataloging-in-Publication Data

Etingoff, Kim.
  The science of the beast : the facts behind the fangs / by Kim Etingoff.
      p. cm.
  Includes bibliographical references (p.   ) and index.
  ISBN 978-1-4222-1808-2 (hardcover) -- ISBN 978-1-4222-1961-4 (pbk.)
  1. Vampires—Juvenile literature. 2. Werewolves—Juvenile literature. I. Title.
  BF1556.E84 2011
  398'.45—dc22
                                          2010023660

Produced by Harding House Publishing Service, Inc.
www.hardinghousepages.com
Interior design by MK Bassett-Harvey.
Cover design by Torque Advertising + Design.
Printed in the USA by Bang Printing.

CONTENTS

chapter I
FEAR AND MONSTERS

Most people suspect that vampires and werewolves aren't real. Not everything about vampires and werewolves is invented, though. The monster myths and legends that we know and repeat today have roots in normal occurrences in the everyday world. Real animals, diseases, and psychological conditions all helped to create the terrifying creatures of folktales, horror movies, and classic books.

The fear we feel when confronted with images or stories that portray vampires and werewolves is certainly real. Fear is an essential part of being human, and a natural response to monsters, real or invented. Fear has been a part of vampire and werewolf stories for a long time, and it's no different today.

Survival Instinct

Although fear can be unpleasant, our lives are a lot better off if we're afraid of some things. In general, people are afraid of objects and events that can hurt them. A creak in the night, a growling animal, or a tap from behind could all potentially be a source of danger. That's not always true—the creak in the night could very well be the wind at your window—but it's better to be safe than sorry. If we're aware and prepared for danger, we can avoid walking into dangerous situations and can survive the ones we do encounter.

The Creation of Fear

What actually happens between the second you hear a strange noise and the second you feel that surge of panic? There's a lot that goes on in that tiny moment. Basically, the noise is the stimulus that triggers your brain to release chemicals that create the physical and emotional feeling of fear. Fear is an autonomic response (a response that isn't consciously controlled), like blinking. Once you perceive a stimulus like a loud noise or an angry animal, a part of the brain called the hypothalamus activates the nervous system. Meanwhile, the hypothalamus also stimulates the adrenal-cortical system in the bloodstream, which simply means that it tells certain glands to release chemicals called adrenaline

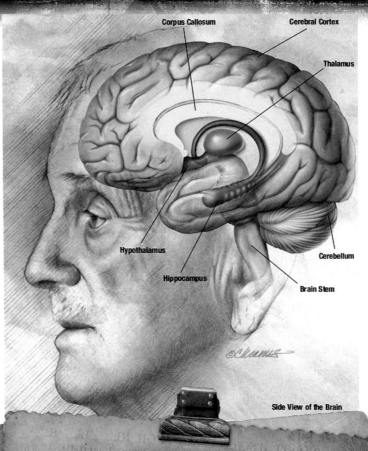

Corpus Callosum

Cerebral Cortex

Thalamus

Hypothalamus

Cerebellum

Hippocampus

Brain Stem

Side View of the Brain

The Hypothalamus

In the center of the brain is a small structure called the hypothalamus. It acts as the control center for all of the automatic processes of the body, such as heartbeat, breathing, and maintenance of body temperature. It also regulates hormones, chemical substances that control and adjust the activity of cells and organs in the rest of the body.

and noradrenalin. All these actions taken together create the familiar physical sensations of fear: a racing heart, tense muscles, a feeling of readiness.

Your body goes through a lot of sudden changes once it senses a stimulus. Besides the increase in heart rate and the tense muscles, your blood pressure also increases, your pupils dilate, blood is sent toward your main muscles, and your digestive and immune systems slow or shut down. All of these reactions are meant to contribute to your ability to deal with whatever is scaring you. Taken together, they make up the fight-or-flight response. Typical of many animals, including humans, the fight-or-flight response means that you're ready to either face the stimulus in front of you—or run away. All that attention your body is paying to its main muscles, for example, will allow you to either fight with strength or run away as fast as possible. A different part of your brain evaluates whether you should fight or flee, since choosing the wrong option blindly could end in injury or death. Your brain can also look at the stimulus causing the fear, and decide that it's nothing to worry about. If that happens, your feelings of fear quickly disappear.

Nurture vs. Nature

Scientists have debated the causes of human behavior for a long time. Some think that most of what we do is determined by natural characteristics and genetics.

LEARNING FEAR

In 1920, two researchers named John B. Watson and Rosalie Rayner conducted an experiment to demonstrate that fear can be learned. In a rather cruel experiment, they conditioned a baby named Little Albert to fear white rats. Albert initially enjoyed playing with the rats, but every time he reached for one, the researchers would play a loud noise behind him. He eventually learned to associate the rats with the loud noise, and became afraid of them whenever he saw them. He learned to fear rats so strongly that he even started to fear other furry animals, along with a Santa Claus beard that probably reminded him of the white rats.

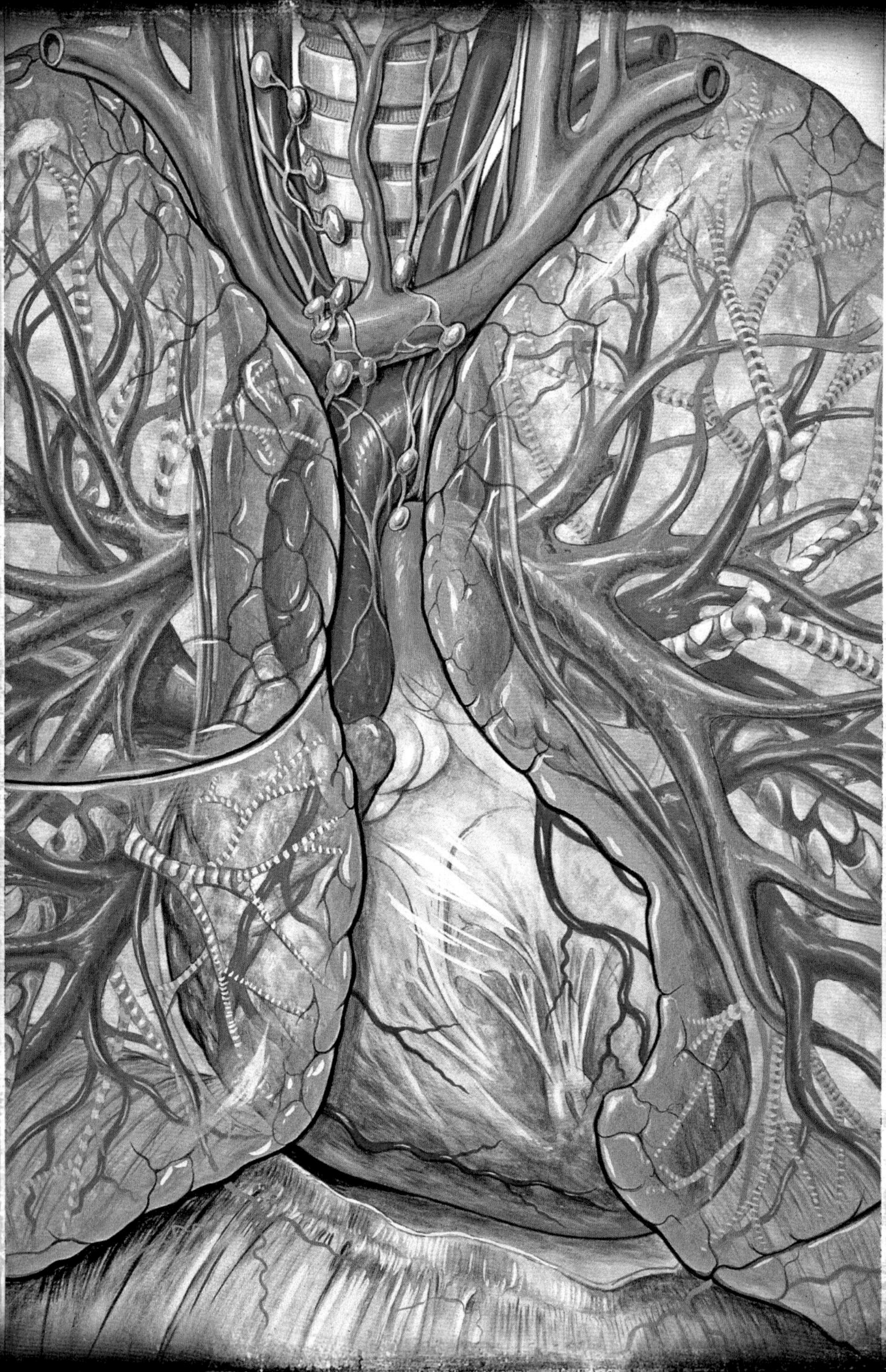

That's the "nature" side of the debate. Other scientists believe that most of our behavior is the result of the environment that we grow up in, the "nurture" position. In reality, human behavior can't really be boiled down to either nurture or nature. Instead, it's a complicated mixture of both.

The same is true of humans' ability to fear. Being afraid is definitely a natural part of being a human being, and almost all people demonstrate some sort of fear response. Fear responses have even been detected in babies as young as seven months old. Think about it: you're probably afraid of some things that you've never even experienced. There's a good chance that you'd be pretty terrified if a bull charged toward you, even though it's likely that you've never been in that situation: you didn't need to learn to be scared in this situation.

That's true for people all over the world. The fact that people fear things they haven't experienced previously suggests that fear must have at least some genetic components. We don't have to learn that a large animal running toward us is dangerous; our body already recognizes that it should start working on that fear response. Additionally, some evidence indicates that people are predisposed to fear certain things that are poisonous

When you are scared, your body undergoes many changes on the inside. Your heart and lungs work faster, blood pressure increases, and the blood flows toward the muscles you will need to either run away or fight.

or that could carry disease. For example, many people are afraid of animals like snakes, rats, and spiders, some species which have the potential to be dangerous.

At the same time, fear also has an element of nurture. We do, in fact, learn to fear certain things. An adult man who is afraid of dogs, for example, might have been bitten by one as a child. Psychology experiments have shown that scientists are able to create fear in subjects (usually animals, but in some cases humans), and to also make fears disappear. Some people with intense fears, called phobias, go to psychologists to learn how to manage their distressing feelings. Usually, psychologists lead people with phobias through a program of exposure. First, the person is shown a picture of the object they fear. Then, they might be put in the same room with the object, which is later brought closer and closer, until the person can touch it. While this process doesn't always work, it does show that fears can, in some cases, be unlearned.

The Fun of Fear

While facing down a grizzly bear might not be most people's idea of fun, many people seek out safer ways to experience fear in an enjoyable way. Horror movies are extremely popular, as are roller coasters and activities like skydiving. Many people enjoy the feeling of adrenaline pumping through their system, as long as they don't have

TAKING FEAR TOO FAR

The fear of vampires is called sanguivoriphobia, which literally means "fear of blood eaters." This phobia takes the form of an intense, irrational fear of vampire creatures. In 1973, the **Ludington Daily News** reported an extreme case of sanguivoriphobia. A man was discovered dead in his English home; he had choked to death on a piece of garlic while sleeping. It turns out he had been so afraid of vampires that one of his many precautions against them was sleeping with a piece of garlic in his mouth. Unfortunately, his phobia proved to be the cause of his death.

to use it to actually fight or run away from danger. It offers a sense of escapism, meaning that experiencing fear from something that isn't real is a way to escape the mundane world and encounter something exciting and exhilarating.

Our fascination with monsters ties in to both these ideas. If we think they aren't real, we're free to be scared of them, whether it's a scary movie or a campfire tale, without having to worry about how we're going to actually fight them or get away from them. They also take us out of the everyday. It's not likely you're going to meet

VAMPIRE EPIDEMIC

In 2002, vampire fever swept through the South African country of Malawi. Rumors that the government was using vampires to collect blood for food traveled through the countryside. The rumors led to stonings and attacks on government officials and other people thought to be plotting with the government. There was no actual evidence that there were vampires collecting blood, but the starvation, lack of aid, and unhappiness with the government created a panic that couldn't be stopped. The vampires weren't flesh and blood, but they did represent the worries and troubles of Malawian citizens.

a vampire or a werewolf walking down the street—but it's fun to imagine a world where you might.

Monster Fear

But what about people who do believe in vampires and werewolves? These creatures are a part of many cultural traditions around the world, and not always just as an object of fun and make-believe. Creating explanations for unexplained events also gives people a sense of comfort. Before we had medical explanations for things (and even today), disease, illness, and death were mysterious and uncontrollable. Using monsters to explain these things gave people a greater sense of control over their lives and shed some light on why things happened; coming up with ways of protecting themselves against the monsters gave them even greater feelings of control.

Beyond that, monsters and fantastic creatures actually do have some basis in science and real life. While science and history might not be able to prove that vampires or werewolves exist, they do explain why they exist as ideas in the first place. Stories about monsters, along with our fear of them, don't just come from nowhere. Like other fears, it's a mix of biological responses to certain things and learned behaviors. Plenty of things in the natural world have served as inspiration for vampire and werewolf folklore. Things that people were innately afraid of, and things they learned to be afraid of, became the foundations for monster myths.

chapter 2
REAL-LIFE MONSTERS

Vampires and werewolves are definitely frightening, but the animals and people that inspired them are too. Some of the most obvious sources for monster myths are real animals—and a few real-life human beings.

The Animal Inspiration Behind Vampires

Vampire Bats

Vampire bats are exactly what their name implies: flying mammals that drink blood. Their favorite victims are generally large livestock like cows and horses, but they have been known to feed on humans from time to time.

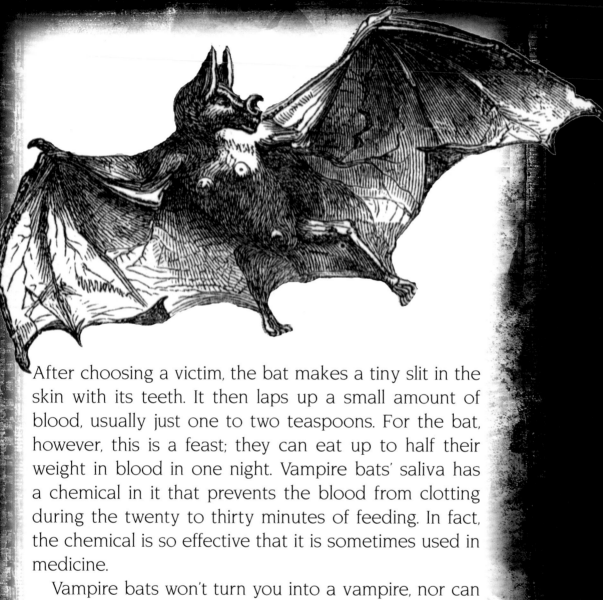

After choosing a victim, the bat makes a tiny slit in the skin with its teeth. It then laps up a small amount of blood, usually just one to two teaspoons. For the bat, however, this is a feast; they can eat up to half their weight in blood in one night. Vampire bats' saliva has a chemical in it that prevents the blood from clotting during the twenty to thirty minutes of feeding. In fact, the chemical is so effective that it is sometimes used in medicine.

Vampire bats won't turn you into a vampire, nor can they kill you by sucking you dry of blood. They take so little blood, and make such a tiny incision in the skin, that most victims don't realize they've been bitten. However, vampire bats can spread disease. They can pass

VAMPIRE BAT SPINOFFS

The habitat of the vampire bat stretches from southern South America through Mexico in the north. The Americas are also home to a number of legends about blood-sucking creatures, perhaps influenced by experiences with vampire bats. The myths include the tlahuelpuchi, which combine werewolf and vampire characteristics. Tlahuelpuchi are witches that turn into coyotes at night, breaking into houses and sucking the blood out of children. Cihuateteo were ancient Aztec vampires who had originally been human women who died in childbirth. After death, they returned to feast on children. In Chile, indigenous beliefs included two creatures called the colo-colo and the pihuechenyi. The colo-colo is a monster that hovers over sleeping bodies, drinking saliva instead of blood. The pihuechenyi is an enormous winged snake that swoops down on sleeping humans to drain them of blood.

on rabies and other diseases through contact between saliva and blood, which makes them very dangerous.

The relationship between vampires and vampire bats is complicated. Many people might think that vampire myths we know today were inspired by the existence of vampire bats, but the opposite is actually true. Vampire bats aren't native to Central and Eastern Europe, where the most well-know vampire legends originated. They are instead native to Central and South America, where they helped to inspire regional variations of the vampire. However, European vampire stories didn't merge with tales of vampire bats until the eighteenth century. Once vampire myths gained popularity and began to travel around the world, stories about European vampires ended up in the Americas. Storytellers there noted that the native bats were awfully similar to vampires—and gave them the name vampire bat.

Other Vampire Creatures

Bats aren't the only animals to drink blood, though they are the only mammals. Mosquitoes are one well-known and pesky blood-drinking insect. Recently, another insect was discovered to rely on a diet of blood; in the last few years, blood-sucking moths have been found in Siberia and other parts of Russia, as well as Southeast Asia and Finland. Not much is known yet about these creatures, but they don't seem to be too dangerous, since they can be kept away with the flick of a hand.

Wolf Names

Several first names from around the world have connections to wolves. Among them are:

Ralph: Counsel Wolf (Germanic)
Guadalupe: Wolf Valley (Spanish)
Lovell: Wolf Cub (French)
Adolf: Noble Wolf (Germanic)
Conall: Wolf Strong (Irish)

They are believed to have come from fruit-eating moths that made the leap to using their proboscises to suck blood instead of nectar.

There is also a vampire bird. The vampire finch of the Galapagos usually eats seeds, insects, and occasionally fruit nectar, but it dines on blood during times of starvation. The finches peck at other, larger birds, drawing blood. The victims don't seem to mind the pecking, perhaps thinking that the finches are merely pecking for parasites.

Other animals bear the name "vampire" even though they don't really drink blood. Vampire squids are small and harmless animals living in the depths of the sea. Their name comes from their eerie appearance rather than their diet. They are black or dark reddish brown, bulbous, and covered with light-producing organs, which help them survive in the dark ocean. They eat small aquatic creatures, not blood.

WERE-ANIMALS

The term werewolf comes from the Old English *were-* or *wer-*, meaning man, plus the name of the animal the man (or woman) turns into. Werewolves aren't the only creatures into which humans can transform. There are were-bears in native North American traditions, were-hares and were-mountain cats in the southern United States, and were-hyenas in Africa. Wolves aren't native to all parts of the New World, so it makes sense that not all cultures have werewolves. Instead, while the idea of transformation stays the same, the animal in question changes based on the part of the world where the myth began.

The vampire squid doesn't really drink blood.

The Predecessors of Werewolves

Wolves are the obvious inspiration behind werewolf stories. The habitat of the wolf coincides with the creation of werewolf legends all over North America and Eurasia. In other parts of the world, other animals stand in for wolves. In South America, for example, there are were-jaguars, which are human beings transformed into jaguars.

Wolves are important animals in many cultures, where they represent power, hunting ability, and fear. Many given names around the world signify "wolf," demonstrating the intimate ties between people and wolves in many societies. Wolves were the first animal to be domesticated as well, probably somewhere in East Asia around 15,000 years ago. Today, their relatives live side-by-side with us in our houses: dogs, man's best friend.

The ambivalent relationship between humans and wolves probably led to the invention of werewolves. On the one hand, people related to wolves and were fascinated by them, but on the other hand, they were afraid of their fearsome nature. Werewolves represent the close, yet dangerous, ties between human beings and wolves. No wonder that tales of wolf-men were told, or that they still hold people's interest today.

Despite the fear wolves aroused because of their teeth, claws, and fierce hunting style, wolves rarely attack humans. They were mostly hated for attacking livestock, which in turn caused starvation for the families that depended on their cows and sheep for survival. There are some reports of wolves stealing children, mainly in India where people have moved into wolves' natural habitats, but most wolf attacks occur because the animals have been driven mad by rabies.

Plants with Power

Animals aren't the only life forms associated with vampires and werewolves. Plants have also been woven into monster stories for centuries. Garlic is perhaps the first plant that comes to mind when thinking of these monsters. It's thought of as a natural protection against vampires, who avoid it at any cost. The link between garlic and vampires is extremely old, originating in Romania and the surrounding region. Although no one knows exactly why people consider garlic to be a powerful plant that can so effectively ward off vampires, it's probably because of its healthful properties. Research and folklore suggest that garlic has cardiovascular benefits and strong antibacterial properties. It may even contribute to cancer prevention. This might not explain why garlic protects specifically against vampires, but it does help explain why garlic, and not another plant, was chosen as a protective tool.

Wolfsbane is a famous plant that has a close connection with werewolves. As its name suggests, it is thought to protect against werewolves. Also known as aconitum and closely related to monkshood, wolfsbane grows mainly in mountainous regions of the northern hemisphere, like the Alps. It is said to repel wolves and werewolves, or sometimes to cause someone to turn into a werewolf. Occasionally, it is thought of as a cure for the werewolf condition. In reality, it is very poisonous and should be avoided by humans as well as wolves!

Gruesome People

The natural world isn't the only source of real-life inspirations for vampires and werewolves. A few people throughout history have also influenced monster myths.

Vlad the Impaler

The most famous person connected to traditional vampire stories is Vlad the Impaler, also known as Dracula. He wasn't a real vampire, because he wasn't a supernatural being that sucked blood, but he was a cruel man. Vlad was a fifteenth-century prince in Wallachia, which is in the Eastern European country of modern-day Romania.

During Vlad's rule, the Ottoman Empire, a large kingdom centered in modern-day Turkey, threatened Wallachia. Vlad fought the Ottomans ruthlessly, and his subjects praised him for keeping them safe. Vlad then turned to restoring order in his own kingdom and began to impale people who stood in his way. He murdered thousands of nobles and commoners, impaling them on stakes as warnings to others. On later military campaigns, he also killed thousands of people, spreading his reputation as a mass murderer. The numbers of people he killed are probably exaggerated, but his actions led to rumors, which became legends. Soon after his death, stories about his deeds spread in pamphlets throughout Europe. In most of the continent, he is demonized as a cruel killer, but in Romania and Eastern Europe, people still take a more kindly view of him, since he freed their ancestors from invaders.

The name Dracula comes from Vlad's father, who was nicknamed "Dracul." The name means "dragon," and was given to his father because he belonged to a royal society called the Order of the Dragons. Dracula means "son of the dragon." The name stuck through history, until it inspired the novelist Bram Stoker in his book, *Dracula*. Stoker had read accounts of vampire legends in Romania, as well as the history of Vlad the Impaler, and he decided to set his story in that region. He invented

many of the fictional Dracula's characteristics, such as his ability to turn into a bat, but he was undoubtedly inspired partly by stories about Vlad Dracula.

A Female Vampire

Another possible inspiration for modern vampire stories is Elizabeth Bathory, a sixteenth-century countess in Hungary. She also may have influenced Stoker's Dracula character, because of her reputation for killing and her focus on blood. Bathory was particularly fond of convincing young girls to come work as maids for her, then torturing and killing them one by one with gruesome methods like starvation, freezing, and mutilation. Although Bathory has never been accused of drinking blood, she is thought to have bathed in it. She is better known for her love of murder and her extreme ways of killing, including biting her victims' flesh. Along with various servants as accomplices, Bathory managed to kill up to 200 girls. Her murders first went unnoticed, but as soon as she started luring young noble girls to her castle, she was put on trial and convicted.

No one knows for sure why Bathory killed so many people, but it may have had to do with mental illness. As a child, she had a terrible temper and convulsive fits, and she later displayed mental imbalance. The nobility at that time in Europe was known for its cruelty to peasants and commoners, and no one really tried to stop Bathory from her crimes, even though there were rumors about them, until she became a threat to the nobility as well.

With people like old Vlad and Elizabeth Bathory on the loose, it's no wonder that whispered rumors grew into darker, more widespread stories. But they weren't the only real-life monsters on the loose.

chapter 3
MONSTER DISEASES

Before the rise of science and medicine, people used the supernatural to explain life's abnormalities and strange events. The vampires and werewolves of today were shaped partly by people's experiences with diseases and physical deformities or abnormalities. Attributing weird appearances and behavior to monsters was an easy way of explaining the unknown.

Vampire Diseases

Porphyria

One disease that is commonly associated with vampirism is porphyria. Porphyria is an illness that interferes with the body's ability to produce haem, a substance that allows the body to use oxygen efficiently. Outward signs of porphyria include sensitivity to light, blistering,

PORPHYRIA: A DISEASE OF THE NOBILITY

Scientists and historians have speculated that many famous people, mostly in Europe, had porphyria. They include King George III and Mary, Queen of Scots. Some historians speculate that because all of the rulers of Europe inbred so often, porphyria was very widespread among European rulers. Vlad the Impaler of Wallachia (today Transylvania), the original, historical basis for Count Dracula, is also rumored to have had porphyria.

scarring, skin darkening, and seizures. It also causes skin and gums to recede, making nails and teeth look dramatically longer. The teeth and fingernails of a sufferer also sometimes turn red, as does urine.

Some of these symptoms seem to match up with traditional signs of vampires. Longer, red teeth and sensitivity to light are two things that could make people

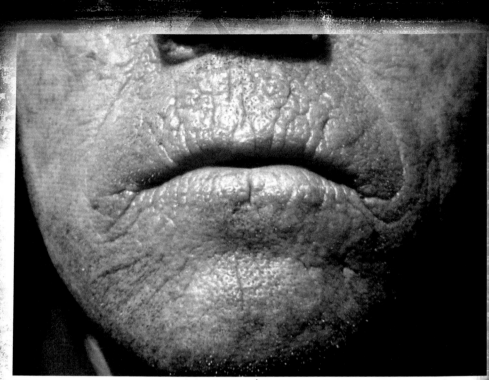

This person with porphyria developed skin lesions from exposure to light.

with porphyria seem like vampires, at least to modern eyes. However, the idea that vampires are afraid of sunlight is relatively new, so it's unlikely that contributed to porphyria fears hundreds of years ago. There's no real evidence yet that porphyria inspired vampire myths, but it certainly is a possibility.

Tuberculosis

Also called consumption, tuberculosis used to be a much-feared disease of the lungs. A diagnosis of tuberculosis meant almost certain death. It also caused alarming changes in appearance, which could have inspired fears of vampires. Tuberculosis victims are pale, with swollen red eyes. Their body temperature drops, making them almost like living corpses. Most chilling, people with tuberculosis cough up blood. Between the supposed evidence of blood sucking and their deathly appearance, it's easy to see why they could have become vampire suspects.

Anemia

Not all diseases made their sufferers into vampires. Sometimes they made them seem like the victims of vampires. Anemia is a blood disease in which there isn't enough red blood cells to carry oxygen to all parts of the body. Today there are many causes of anemia, including iron deficiency, chronic diseases like AIDS, genetic inheritance, and environmental factors. A person with anemia looks a lot like a vampire victim might: pale, tired all the time, short of breath, dizzy, with cold hands and feet. Not having enough oxygen in your blood is pretty similar to having less blood in your body overall, since one of the main functions of blood is impaired by not having enough red blood cells.

The Bite of the Werewolf

Rabies

At least one disease probably inspired werewolf tales around the world. Rabies is a widespread disease passed

A RABIES SURVIVOR

Once symptoms of rabies show up, there is no known treatment. However, there have been a handful of survivors in the last few years. In 2004, a young girl was bitten by a bat she found in her church. A month later, the girl was taken to the hospital with some of the symptoms of rabies, and the disease soon took over her body. Her doctor came up with a novel and risky procedure to try and save her life by inducing a coma. The idea was to protect her brain from damage while her immune system created antibodies to fight the virus in her blood; usually the body doesn't have time to do this before the disease causes death. A mixture of luck, treatment, and a strong immune system combined to prevent her death. Although she had to relearn how to walk and talk, today she is a normal girl who attends college.

on to humans by bites from infected animals. The virus causes inflammation of the brain, which results in dis-orientation, hydrophobia (the fear of water), a desire to be left alone, and delirium. People infected with rabies also have urges to attack and bite other people.

Bats and wolves both carry rabies, along with a host of other mammals. Today, people who have been bitten

MODERN-DAY WOLF MAN

Jesús "Chuy" Aceves, from Zacatecas, Mexico, is the second person in his family born with hypertrichosis. Chuy's face is covered with hair, making him resemble the legendary wolf man or, as some call him, a monkey man. Chuy is married and has two daughters, one of whom also has the condition. His sister Lili does as well. In 2005, Jesús shaved for the first time for the BBC documentary *It's Not Easy Being a Wolf Boy*. He had been working most of his life for a carnival's freak show, and he hoped to get a "regular" job so he could work near his home, and not leave his family for long periods of time. Unfortunately, the pay of a regular job was not as good as that in a freak show or circus. In 2007, Chuy was featured in the books *Ripley's Believe It or Not!* and *Guinness World Records*.

by possibly rabid animals can be vaccinated against the disease. There is no cure once symptoms appear, usually a few weeks to two years after the bite, but vastly fewer deaths occur from rabies today than in the past.

Rabies must have been an extremely scary disease before there were preventative measures, since it turned people into raving monsters. The connection between animals like wolves and rabies is significant, and probably contributed to a sense of the often-dangerous connection between animals and humans, along with fear of animals that could pass along rabies.

Hypertrichosis

Hypertrichosis is more easily remembered by the catchier names of wolfitis, or werewolf syndrome. This disease quite literally turns people into creatures that look like werewolves, though they are definitely still human. Hypertrichosis causes excessive hair growth on the body and face, though it doesn't have any ill health effects.

There are several types of hypertrichosis. All babies are covered in downy hair in the womb, but they usually lose it before birth. A few children are born with some of this hair left, which is a mild form of hypertrichosis. In other cases, it keeps growing throughout life. The most extreme cases involve normal hair—like what's on your head—growing all over the body, including the face.

People with hypertrichosis used to be destined for circuses, labeled as "wolf men" in sideshows. The

This European artwork from the Middle Ages reveals that hypertrichosis was a known condition even then.

first person recorded to have had hypertrichosis was Petrus Gonzales, a man born in the Canary Islands in 1556. He was taken to the French court where he lived as a curiosity. He was also given an education at court and reportedly led a satisfying life. Since then, several people and families have been noted as having hyper-trichosis. The most famous case right now is the Aceves family in Mexico.

Hypertrichosis can't be cured, but it can be controlled with physical or chemical methods of hair removal. However, some people with hypertrichosis today have accepted their condition and lead fairly normal lives. Today, we also understand the medical explanations for hypertrichosis—but before modern medicine, people with the disease seemed frightening, mysterious, and not quite human. Though they weren't especially violent, it's easy to see why they might have been ostracized as wolf men or werewolves.

Mass Hysteria and Monster Hunts

Food Poisoning

In the medieval period of European history, monster hunts were quite common. Entire towns would be swept up in the fear of vampires, werewolves, or witches. Thousands of people were killed, accused of being monsters.

A number of reasons contributed to this sort of mass hysteria. Many times, a town would be experiencing a period of famine or disease. They didn't understand what was causing so much sickness and death, nor did they have any control over it. Witchcraft, sorcery, or vampirism made sense as the cause of terrible events, and allowed townspeople the feeling that they could take action rather than sit around and do nothing.

Another intriguing theory behind mass hysteria is ergot poisoning. Ergot is a small fungus that grows on rye plants, which could be found in flour and bread in medieval times. Farmers would harvest the rye without removing the fungus and grind it up into flour for rye bread. At that time, rye bread was a staple in peasant diets all over Europe, so people ended up eating quite a lot of the fungus.

There are two types of ergot poisoning. In convulsive poisoning, the ergot causes fits, muscle spasms, and twisting of the body. It looks like victims are going crazy. Gangrenous poisoning constricts blood vessels in arms and legs, leading to infection and eventually loss of limbs because of lack of blood. Either of these two appearances of ergot poisoning could have seemed like witchcraft. Sometimes entire towns would suffer from the same symptoms, causing alarm and suffering. People knew that something must have been behind the convulsions and gangrene, so they turned to supernatural explanations like witchcraft.

Ergot poisoning was a truly terrible disease, because no one really knew what was causing it or how to prevent it. Farmers kept harvesting infected rye, and families kept baking poisoned loaves of bread. Even if someone recovered from ergot poisoning, they often just reinfected themselves by eating more ergot.

It wasn't until 1670 that a French doctor, Dr. Thuillier, began to investigate the cause of the poisoning. He noticed that only rural, poor people got sick. He also saw that sometimes only one person in a household suffered, or sometimes people who lived all alone, isolated from other communities. He concluded that it was something to do with people's diets, rather than witchcraft or an infectious disease. He eventually figured out that the little fungus on rye bread was causing the sickness, though his conclusions did little to sway people's beliefs. It would take 200 more years before ergot was proven to cause the poisoning.

Digging Up Vampires

Vampirism specifically was also used to explain clusters of death and disease. When large numbers of people died at once, such as when an infectious disease like tuberculosis would sweep through an area, survivors were left to wonder why so many people had died. The first person to have died would sometimes be suspected of being a vampire, and thus the cause of the rest of the deaths. The body would be dug up and examined for signs of being a vampire. If the body wasn't decomposed, if it was plump and swollen, or had liquid blood around the mouth and nose, the vampire hunters would ritually kill the body again. They would accomplish this by cutting off the head, driving a stake through the heart, or removing the heart and burning it.

Dead people were believed to be vampires if they looked healthy and if there was evidence of their blood feasts. However, the state of corpses depends on how they were buried and what they died from. For example, certain temperatures can keep bodies preserved rather than decomposed. Gases build up in dead bodies, leaving them plumper than when they were first buried, and escaping gases can make dead bodies moan, just like monsters. Gases can also force blood up through the mouth and nose. Skin and nails fall off, leaving what looks like new skin underneath. All in all, dead bodies can look remarkably lifelike, if they are dug up fairly quickly.

One famous vampire hunt occurred in the United States in 1892. Immediately before that year, the town of Exeter, Rhode Island, had experienced an outbreak of tuberculosis. A number of people died, including a nineteen-year-old girl named Mercy Brown, along with her mother and older sister. Mercy's brother also sickened, prompting her father to take action. He and other townspeople suspected a vampire to be behind the recent deaths, and as Mercy and her mother and sister had been among the first deaths, their bodies were dug up. The mother and sister had decomposed, but Mercy had not. Her fresh appearance and the liquid blood found in her heart seemed to prove that she was a vampire, rising from the dead to victimize her brother. Her father had her heart burned, then mixed the ashes with water to give to her brother to drink. This was

supposed to kill the vampire and save the brother, but unfortunately, he died soon after.

How to Spot a Vampire

Vampire Characteristics

Sometimes a person's physical characteristics determined whether others thought of him or her as a vampire. In medieval Europe, people with sharp tongues or long canine teeth were suspected and ostracized. Those who deviated from mainstream society or displayed antisocial behavior were also suspicious. Prostitutes, alcoholics, and murderers were all misfits in life, and were thought to become vampires after death.

Baby Vampires

There are many old European beliefs that link certain physical characteristics at birth with being a vampire. This meant that some babies were doomed to be labeled as vampires, even before they could walk!

A small percentage of babies are born with a few of their first teeth poking through the gums. In the past, parents and older community members immediately suspected the baby was a vampire, especially if only the two top canine teeth were the ones growing in. In Slavic folklore, babies born with blue eyes and red hair could grow up to be vampires, as might babies born with lots of hair or certain types of birthmarks. Babies born between Christmas and Epiphany (January 6) also had a higher chance of being a vampire than babies born at other times. Other suspicious babies included seventh sons with only male siblings, illegitimate children, and premature babies.

But not all people are destined from birth to be a vampire; sometimes psychological disorders that showed up later in life doomed them. Besides physical characteristics, abnormalities, and diseases, psychological disorders also inspired vampire and werewolf stories.

chapter 4
MODERN-DAY WOLF MAN

Vampire and werewolf stories exist all over the world. Many were created independently of each other, in isolated places. In the past few hundred years, monster stories have traveled around the world as well, changing and shifting as they meet new cultures. But despite the variations on the stories, some common links connect vampire and werewolf stories worldwide. Why is it that these sorts of monsters are so popular and so scary to billions of people? Although the details of the stories vary and are clearly culture-specific, the themes of blood-sucking and shape-shifting seem to transcend cultural differences.

One psychiatrist named Carl Jung came up with a theory to explain why monster stories are so common. He believed that all human beings share some experiences, like birth and death. Because we are all the same species, our brains also interpret those experiences in similar ways. He called his idea the theory of collective unconscious, meaning that people everywhere understand the world in similar ways, although they do so unconsciously. Parallels among myths and folklore are examples of how humans take the same types of experiences and understand them in similar ways. Vampires and werewolves are two monsters that demonstrate this idea. They are generally thought of as reactions to fear, death, and darkness. It isn't surprising that humans everywhere interpret these themes similarly around the world.

Real Werewolves

Lycanthropy is a term that refers to the physical transformation of a person into a werewolf. It is also a medical term for several psychological symptoms of a psychosis, and is more commonly known as "werewolfism." People with lycanthropy believe that they can turn into animals, usually wolves. Symptoms include schizophrenic behavior, depression, and violent behavior. So far, no specific disease has been found that causes lycanthropy; instead, it's a set of behaviors that can be treated with therapy. It is, however, associated with schizophrenia, bipolar disorder, brain tumors, and epilepsy.

A study of a woman suffering from lycanthropy was published in *The American Journal of Psychiatry* in 1977. The

case involved a forty-nine-year-old woman with low self-esteem and an obsession with wolves. At a family gathering, she ripped off her clothes and began acting like a wolf. After a little while, she regained her sense of her human self, but the next night, she again felt herself becoming a wolf. This time, she spent two hours in her bedroom, growling, scratching, and chewing at the bed. By the time the woman was admitted to a hospital, she was hearing voices and claiming she was possessed by the devil. She told the doctors she was a human during the day and a wolf at night. Additionally, she claimed she could see the reflection of a wolf head instead of her own when she looked in the mirror.

The woman was diagnosed with lycanthropy and schizophrenia, and underwent a program of psychotherapy and medication. Fortunately, it worked; she stopped seeing a wolf in the mirror and no longer felt that she was periodically turning into a wolf. This particular woman was lucky that she didn't attack and hurt anyone. Lycanthropy can be a potentially dangerous problem, both for the victim and for people around the victim.

Real Vampires

Clinical Vampirism

Renfield's syndrome is the vampiric equivalent of lycanthropy. People with Renfield's believe they are vampires

and may act on their beliefs. Named after a character in Bram Stoker's classic vampire novel, *Dracula*, the
syndrome is a set of behavioral and emotional symptoms, rather than a specific disease. It's encountered far
more in literature and movies than it is in actual medical
settings.

Most sufferers, real and fictional, are male. They
believe that by ingesting blood they will gain power and
strength. Sometimes this takes the form of auto-vam-
pirism, the need to drink one's own blood. Milder forms
simply involve blood-drinking fantasies, but extreme
variations might lead to drinking others' blood, or even
cannibalism.

Social Vampires

All of the attention being paid to vampires these days
has exposed more and more people to vampire myths
and legends. Some people have become so interested
in these monsters that they want to live like them. The
imitation of vampires comes in many forms. At the
one end are people who enjoy the feeling of stepping
outside the ordinary, pretending to be a vampire in a
role-playing game or at a vampire-themed party. At
the other extreme are people who have become so
attached to vampires that they think actually think they
are vampires. In between is blood play, a controversial
activity that involves group rituals based on blood.

Blood play can mean several different things, though it usually refers to gatherings of two or more people who use blood to fulfill feelings of pleasure or sexual urges. It can involve cutting yourself or others and drinking blood. People who do it claim it is a healthy activity and not a sign of mental illness; they insist it is a healthy way to release anxiety and deal with emotional distress, as long as everyone involved in the blood play is consenting. Others argue that blood play falls outside of the range of normal ways to deal with distress. Furthermore, it is quite dangerous. Sharing blood can pass along blood-born diseases such as HIV/AIDS, and can hurt people who aren't really willing to go along with the process.

A few people take role-playing vampires too far. In a recent case, a group of teenagers pretending to be vampires actually killed two people. The Kentucky teens took an online role-playing game too seriously and decided to live like vampires all the time. They dressed like vampires, slept during the day, and practiced blood play. The group eventually took a trip to the Florida home of the group leader's girlfriend. They initiated her into their cult, and then attacked and killed her parents, leaving them with "V's" burned into their bodies. The teens were found guilty in a court of law, and their leader was sentenced to the death penalty, although the sentence was later reduced to life without parole.

It's hard to define what is art or fashion and what is pathological illness. Explanations of vampires and werewolves have changed over time as well. Behavior that used to be attributed to supernatural monsters is now categorized as mental illness or deviant behavior.

That hasn't stopped vampire and werewolf stories from being as popular, with new movies, books, and TV shows about these creatures popping up every day. The excitement and fear they inspire isn't likely to disappear any time soon. Odds are good that vampires and werewolves will continue to be a part of people's lives all over the world.

WORDS YOU MAY NOT KNOW

accomplices: Companions in wrongdoing, especially ones who aid or abet another in a criminal act.

ambivalent: Simultaneous and contradictory attitudes or feelings (as when you're both attracted to something and grossed out by it at the same time).

antibacterial: Having to do with killing germs or keeping them from growing.

bipolar disorder: A psychological disorder in which a person has periods of depression alternating with periods of mania—intense excitement, hyperactivity, and sometimes delusions—as well as periods of normal mood.

bulbous: Round, swollen, and bulb-shaped.

cardiovascular: Having to do with the heart and the blood vessels.

chronic: Lasting for a long period of time or marked by frequent recurrence, as with certain diseases.

consenting: Agreeing, approving.

controversial: Causing disagreements, as people hold strong and opposite views on something.

decompose: Rot, decay, break down.

deficiency: Not having enough of something, especially something that is necessary to be healthy, like a nutrient.

delirium: A state of mental confusion in which a person can be very excited, incoherent, or can hallucinate, seeing or hearing things that aren't there.

demonized: Represented as evil.

deviated: Turned away from an accepted path or way of doing things.

disorientation: Losing track of time and place and your surroundings.

domesticated: Tamed; brought into a house and taught to live there.

epilepsy: A medical condition causing seizures.

genetics: The branch of biology that deals with heredity.

inbred: Descended from parents who were related to each other. Inbreeding can cause a greater amount of genetic disorders, since parents have many characteristics and genetic traits in common.

indigenous: Something that was born, grew, and lived naturally in a particular region or environment.

infectious: Able to be spread from one person to another, like a disease.

inflammation: Swelling caused by increased blood flow to an injured or sick part of the body, as the body's immune system tries to heal or repair the injury.

innately: Having to do with something that is present in a person's nature or character from birth and does not have to be learned.

irrational: Not governed by reason.

mass hysteria: A condition in which many people are caught up in excitement and fear coming from a false belief that they all share.

medieval: Having to do with the Middle Ages, the period of European history that began in the fifth century and ended in the fifteenth century.

mutilation: Injuring someone by cutting off a part of her body.

ostracized: Excluded from a group.

parasites: Organisms that grow, feed, and are sheltered on or in a different organism, while contributing nothing to the survival of the host.

pathological: Having to do with or caused by disease.

predisposed: Having a likeliness to have certain characteristics, such as behaving in a certain way under certain circumstances.

preventative: Having to do with something that stops something else from happening.

psychosis: Feature of mental illness typically characterized by extreme changes in personality, the inability to function normally, and a distorted or nonexistent sense of what's real.

psychotherapy: A kind of therapy for mental or emotional disorders that involves helping the patient talk about the problems to discover and come to terms with the things that have caused the disorder.

schizophrenic: Relating to a severe mental disorder characterized by delusions, hallucinations, incoherent speech, and physical agitation

speculate: Make educated guesses without enough evidence to prove the guess true.

stimulus: Something that causes a response.

syndrome: A group of symptoms that, when they happen together, are evidence of a certain disorder.

therapy: The treatment of an illness or disorder.

victimize: To harm someone and make them into a victim.

Find Out More on the Internet

Carl Jung
www.nndb.com/people/910/000031817

How Stuff Works: Fear
health.howstuffworks.com/humannature/emotions/other/fear.htm

Monstropedia
www.monstropedia.org/index.php?title=Main_Page

Vampire Bats
animals.nationalgeographic.com/animals/mammals/common-vampire-bat

The Vampire Library
www.vampirelibrary.com

Further Reading

Izzard, Jon. *Werewolves.* London, UK: Spruce, 2009.

Melton, J. Gordon. *The Vampire Book: The Encyclopedia of the Undead.* New York: Visible Ink Press, 2008.

Montague, Charlotte. *Vampires from Dracula to Twilight: the Complete Guide to Vampire Mythology.* New York: Chartwell, 2010.

Steiger, Brad. *The Werewolf Book: The Encyclopedia of Shape-Shifting Beings.* New York: Visible Ink Press, 2009.

Stevenson, Jay. *The Complete Idiot's Guide to Vampires.* Indianapolis, Ind.: Alpha, 2009.

Bibliography

Blumenthal, Ralph. "A Fear of Vampires Can Mask a Fear of Something Much Worse." *New York Times*. 29 Dec. 2002.

"Ergot of Rye- I: Introduction and History." www.botany. hawaii.edu/faculty/wong/bot135/lect12.htm. (26 May 2010).

Izzard, Jon. *Werewolves*. London: Spruce, 2009.

Layton, Julia. "How Fear Works." *How Stuff Works*. 2010. health. howstuffworks.com/human-nature/emotions/other/fear. htm. (25 May 2010).

"Man's Fear of Vampires Causes Death." *Ludington Daily News*. 10 Jan. 1973. news.google.com/newspapers?nid=110 &dat=19730110&id=GasvAAAAIBAJ&sjid=REwDAAAAIBAJ &pg=5426,754180. (25 May 2010).

Montague, Charlotte. *Vampires from Dracula to Twilight: the Complete Guide to Vampire Mythology*. New York: Chartwell, 2010.

National Geographic.com. 2010. www.nationalgeographic. com.

Stevenson, Jay. *The Complete Idiot's Guide to Vampires*. Indianapolis, Ind.: Alpha, 2009.